This book belongs to

CHRISTMAS AT GUMP'S

MIMI McALLISTER

Illustrations by Marion Keen

C. SALWAY PRESS

Written with love, for: Alex, Jeff, and Tom

And four, very special thank-yous to:
Liz Manning, Bonnie Mickelson, Ann Seymour, and Tom Owen

GUMP'S is a registered trademark of Gump's Inc., 250 Post Street,
San Francisco, California 94108. Use of the trademark GUMP'S in this
book is under license from Gump's Inc. There is no connection between
Gump's Inc. and the author or illustrator of this book, apart from the
trademark license. Please contact Gump's for any question regarding use of
the trademark GUMP'S.

ISBN 0-9624887-4-7
Library of Congress Catalog Card Number: 90-60435
First Edition
Book design: Seventeenth Street Studios
Printed in Hong Kong
Second Printing

C. Salway Press
P.O. Box 4115
Menlo Park, CA 94026

IT WAS the Christmas season and something very exciting was happening in downtown San Francisco.

The Society for the Prevention of Cruelty to Animals (S.P.C.A.) had joined with Gump's famous home-furnishing store in an extraordinary experiment to find loving homes for the city's stray and abandoned animals. Their clever plan was to replace Gump's traditional window displays with irresistible pets from the S.P.C.A. kennels.

Gump's had thoughtfully offered to decorate the windows to make certain their little S.P.C.A. guests would feel welcome. At the same time, they hoped to remind all the passers-by that these and other homeless pets had a special Christmas wish . . .
for a new family to love.

These "guest rooms" turned out to be a delightful surprise for the entire Bay Area. Who wouldn't be thrilled to find adorable cats, kittens, puppies and dogs clowning, chasing, tumbling, wrestling, and sometimes snoozing in the holiday windows!

In addition to plenty of food and water, colorful curtains, rugs, wallpaper, pictures, dressing tables, and even miniature beds were placed in each charming window. And, of course, lots of toys were added to keep everyone entertained . . . on BOTH sides of the glass. Each day, S.P.C.A. volunteers were close by to help the new owners select a pet and to explain that caring for their cat or dog would be a lifelong responsibility.

This innovative use of Gump's windows was not only a brilliant idea, but an overwhelming success. By Christmas Eve, all the lucky animals were warm and snug in their new homes.

All, except for six: Fred, Yvonne, Ruffie, C.C., Monica, and Snow.

But don't worry. They didn't mind spending a little more time in the cozy "guest rooms"; their new owners were coming for them the day after Christmas.

Fred and Yvonne, the two lively dogs, were looking forward to flying to Texas on a big airplane with their new family: a cheery mother and father, who owned a health spa near Dallas, and their twins.

Ruffie, C.C., Monica, and Snow, the four spunky cats, could hardly wait to go live with the groundskeeper at a nearby golf course. What fun they would have romping all over the grass! Ruffie even thought they could practice writing in the sand traps when no one was looking.

This is a story about these six friends:

FRED is a Dalmatian dog with a whole bunch of black spots that he calls "Fred's funny freckles." He claims to be very brave, full of pep, fun to be with—just an all-around great guy!

YVONNE, Fred's best friend, is a sweet-natured, Old English sheepdog with five pounds of gray and white shaggy fur. She found a pair of sunglasses at the beach and likes to wear them on her forehead to keep the hair out of her eyes.

RUFFIE is a striped tabby cat with long, white legs. He got his name because of all his brothers and sisters, he was the champion rough-houser. Ruffie thinks he has outgrown that name and is going to introduce himself as "MacRuffie" the minute he gets to the golf course. He loves everything—especially languages, art, and traveling.

C.C. is a boy cat with a peculiar name. He doesn't remember how he got that name, but he's sure it means "Clever Cat." C.C. is a Siamese with bright blue eyes. When he's not curled up napping in a favorite bowl, he performs acrobatic stunts and makes everyone laugh.

MONICA is a very curious calico cat. She was named for someone's great-aunt. (Do you know any great-aunts with orange, black, and white hair?) Monica goes exploring every chance she gets, so sometimes she's even late for meals and bedtime.

SNOW was so fluffy and white as a kitten, she looked like a real snowball. People always say, "My, what a pretty cat," but Snow would prefer to be a tabby like Ruffie. It's such a bother having to keep clean all the time. She has a funny sense of humor and still likes to play with balls.

CHAPTER ONE

FRED STARED in amazement as the door to their "guest room" swung slowly ajar. Suddenly, he could see a glimpse of Gump's magnificent interior through the narrow crack.

"The lock on our door must be broken," Fred gasped in delight.

With a nudge, he quickly awakened Yvonne, wiggled across the floor and quietly pushed on the handle. Not a soul in sight!

Fred jumped down onto the showroom floor.

Yvonne followed right behind him.

"The cats, Fred! The cats should see this too!" whispered Yvonne in disbelief.

Fred gleefully bounded over to the cats' window. Stretching as tall as he could, he skillfully unlocked their door. You see, he was quite the escape artist with lots of practice opening backyard gates. Fred had routinely roamed his old neighborhood, much to his former owner's dismay.

The clanking noise startled three of the four cats. It was Snow who kept right on dreaming. She was very comfy in her favorite spot, the miniature four-poster bed.

Greatly relieved to see Fred's funny freckled face, Ruffie, C.C., and Monica raced to their newly opened door and peered out.

There, silhouetted in the dim light, was the most beautiful Christmas tree they had ever seen. It was so big that all the ornaments were real toys and real musical instruments. Hanging from the tall ceiling were huge colored rings that looked just like giant Life-Savers. And perched inside them was a whole zoo of stuffed animals.

"G-G-Gosh, would you look at that!" Fred stammered, as he pointed to a life-sized Dalmatian dog swinging right above his head.

Everywhere they looked were gifts. Gold and white Christmas boxes tied with red bows were stacked high. As far as they could see were holiday tables full of things like Japanese parasols, handpainted bunnies from Hungary, English trays with pictures of horses and dogs, and fragile-looking bird cages from Thailand.

Snow rubbed her eyes and sleepily joined the stunned little group. "Is this a dream, too?" she murmured.

"No Snow, you're not dreaming. This really and truly is happening," said Ruffie and he gave her a playful pinch to prove it.

FRED, YVONNE, RUFFIE, C.C., MONICA, AND SNOW WERE ALL ALONE IN A DESERTED DEPARTMENT STORE ON CHRISTMAS DAY!!!!!

CHAPTER TWO

FRED AND RUFFIE quickly realized that this remarkable turn of events might even be a story to tell their children some day!

"Why don't we each take a partner and go roaming?" Fred suggested.

"Great idea, Fred! This is the chance of a lifetime," added Ruffie.

Snow was giggling, "Our new families will never believe this, but isn't it fun?" Monica and Yvonne agreed.

C.C. did one of his crazy somersaults and reminded his pals, "Since it's Christmas, the store will be closed and we can prowl around for hours."

"Race you up those stairs, Fred! Let's hurry and see how high we can go," said Ruffie, sneaking a head start.

"Well, sure thing, neighbor!" yelped Fred as his pal Yvonne gave him a helpful shove. Yvonne had pushed her sunglasses back up to make sure she wouldn't miss anything.

Ruffie was the bravest of the cats. He was also their self-appointed leader. C.C., Monica and Snow were really quite fond of him and cheered loudly as he bolted up the stairs two at a time.

Before Ruffie disappeared from sight, he called back, "Let's meet back here in fifteen minutes so we can all tell about our favorite finds!" Off they scattered.

C.C. and Yvonne both wanted to go up to the second floor to get a better look at the very tip-top of a tree that was two stories high. They also thought they saw something glittering up there.

Monica and Snow decided to check out the whole first floor and dashed off to their right, glancing briefly at a collection of Oriental knickknacks, lacquered bowls, and kimonos.

"Look out!" Snow screamed a warning to Monica. Too late! Monica ran straight into a gigantic wooden turtle that had to be at least three times her size.

"Ouch," Monica laughed and rubbed her nose. "Why didn't I 'hurdle' that turtle? Ho, ho, ho."

They scooted around the next corner and found themselves inside the enormous Fancy Food Department. Good heavens, what a sight! Lots of colorful tins and boxes, jars and bottles. And the names— nothing familiar here!

"Wouldn't Ruffie love this? He's so smart, I just know he could tell us what everything is," said Snow.

Although Monica and Snow couldn't sniff any pet food, they did find some Italian biscotti cookies in orange and white bags, red pasta noodles, tomato paste in toothpaste tubes, olive oils in tin cans, and even some skinny bottles of vinegar with weeds growing inside.

From France, there were cans of oysters, goose liver, and snails!

Next, they saw a table full of water crackers, berry jams, orange marmalades, and teas from England.

From here in Northern California, there were braided ropes of
garlic, strings of black and red chiles, jars of artichoke hearts, golden
mustards, teeny ears of corn, and something really weird . . .
"sun-dried tomatoes."

Snow couldn't resist jumping up on a glass case to play with some
brown balls on a silver platter. She accidentally bumped into the plate,
and just as the balls rolled off the counter onto the floor, she saw the sign,
"Chocolate Truffles."

Snow quickly hopped down and lined up a few of the skinny vinegar
bottles like ten-pins, making a bowling alley. As she was rolling the
bumpy, brown balls down the carpet she couldn't resist shouting "Strike!"
to her imaginary fans.

Monica had ventured around the corner, more slowly this time, and discovered the breath-taking Jewelry Department. This room was just the opposite of the Fancy Food Department, she thought. Very calm, very elegant, and probably very expensive.

Only a few of the jewelry cases were unlocked, but Monica wasted no time trying on everything that would fit around her tiny neck. The watches and bracelets made terrific looking collars, and the necklaces were perfect belts. The clip-on earrings were fun, too.

"Snow, Dahling, do come see my new collar! It's just a little trinket I picked out for everyday wear on the golf course," teased Monica.

CHAPTER THREE

There was a sudden flurry of activity
throughout the store.

Fred and Ruffie charged around the
third floor, Snow bowled, Monica tried on
jewelry, and Yvonne had clambered up the
stairs. All the while, the agile C.C. was
still eyeing the towering Christmas
tree . . . .

Then, just as Yvonne reached the
second floor, Clever Cat could stand it
no longer and scrambled halfway up the
trunk and swayed back and forth.

"I don't care if you ARE a Siamese
cat, you'll break your neck, you silly goose!"
screeched a terrified Yvonne.

So, Clever Cat abandoned his
not so clever shortcut and tried the stairs.

Then together, the two explorers
stood in awe for several minutes. But
soon, Yvonne and C.C.'s heads were like
little swivels trying to see everything at once.

On their right were several different rooms. The signs didn't help too much: Baccarat (Bock-a-rah), Lalique (Lah-LEEK), Steuben (Stew-BEN), Herend (Hair-end).

But the names were so tempting, Yvonne and C.C. had to take a closer look. The shimmering tables and glass shelves looked like a sea of Fourth of July sparklers. They were filled with imported crystal: bowls, candlesticks, lamps, water goblets, ice buckets, and even a few golf balls.

And lots more animals: seals, frogs, ducks, sea-otters, penguins, rabbits, doves, bears, parrots, mice, eagles, horses, fish, giraffes, zebras, monkeys, a sleek jaguar, more turtles, and two smug looking camels.

C.C. leapt onto a beautiful table and meandered gracefully AROUND and OVER and IN the delicate crystal—lastly, he tried out all the punch bowls for nap-size.

"It's a good thing you've had so much experience, C.C. It would be awful if you tripped over one of those valuable gifts and broke it!" said Yvonne.

C.C. appeared not to hear.

Yvonne trotted over to him and gently tilted C.C.'s tiny head up with her huge fluffy paws. "Look at that, C.C., there must be hundreds of stuffed animals in those colored rings hanging from the ceiling," she said.

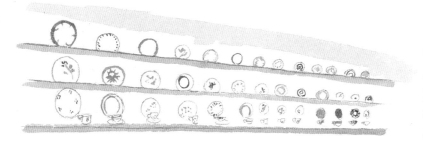

"Gosh, don't they remind you of acrobats at the circus?" C.C. laughed and jumped up to grab a beige and brown Siamese cat dangling by a paw. "I don't like heights as much as he does, Yvonne," C.C. spoofed.

"Yvonne," he continued, "I feel just like Dorothy in the 'Wizard of Oz.' Do you remember when she entered the Emerald City and saw all those fabulous sights at the same time?"

"To be honest, C.C., you really look more like Goldilocks trying out all the cereal bowls," laughed Yvonne, and she made a bee-line for the rows of pretty, china plates that lined the back wall.

Yvonne couldn't resist picking up a sparkling-white dinner plate with a blue border. She was startled to see another "Yvonne" looking back at her with the same surprised expression!

In a flash, she had a sensational idea. Yvonne actually chuckled out loud, she was so pleased with herself.

She scurried back to the holiday table and tenderly scooped C.C. out of his vantage point in a crystal punch bowl. "You'll never believe what I just thought of, C.C.! Let's hurry back downstairs so I can tell everyone at the same time."

Yvonne's huge black eyes were twinkling with excitement.

CHAPTER FOUR

Wʜᴇɴ ꜰʀᴇᴅ and Ruffie reached the third floor they didn't know which way to turn first. It was full of furniture and seemed more spread out than the second floor. In one corner, Ruffie spied a splendid art gallery. There was even an alcove full of Zuñi Indian things from New Mexico.

Fred plopped a wild-looking, feathered headdress on his head just for fun. It was too big, but he still thought it fit his image as a "chief". He raised his right paw and, in a deep voice, growled "HOW!" at poor Ruffie.

Ruffie, pretending to be frightened, loped off towards the art gallery. He didn't want to waste one more minute.

Something made him glance back . . . just in time to see Fred poised to do a few warm-up exercises on a nearby sofa.

Ruffie hurriedly called a reminder to Fred, "Please don't get lost or fall asleep somewhere so you miss our meeting. It's in thirteen minutes—and we'd better be on time."

Fred was distracted. The whole third floor looked like ONE GIANT TRAMPOLINE.

The delirious Dalmatian was soon bouncing from sofa to chair and from chair to sofa.

"Wa-hoo!" No one was even trying to shoo him off.

Boink! Thump! Bonk! Splat! Plomp! Thronk! Bimph! Splink!

Poor Ruffie shuddered and covered his eyes as Fred catapulted out of sight.

Once again, Ruffie started off to spend some quiet time in the art gallery. Soon he chose the perfect spot and climbed up on a bench. It was right smack in front of a Pablo Picasso (Pick-aw-so) etching, a Georges Braque (Brawk) lithograph, a David Hockney watercolor, and a Richard Diebenkorn graphic. Quite extraordinary for a store. This looked more like a museum, Ruffie thought.

It wasn't long before he was imagining himself visiting all the faraway art galleries he had only heard about. The Louvre (Loov-ruh), Jeu de Paume (Joo-duh-Poam), Musée d'Orsay (Moo-zay door-say), in Paris, France; the Prado (Praw-doh) in Madrid, Spain; the Tate (Tayt) and National Galleries in London, England. Ruffie was especially lucky because his former owner had been an art teacher and pets always learn so much from their families.

With a start, Ruffie realized he had been sitting and staring for a long while. "That's not fair," he thought to himself. "The time went by much too fast!"

Reluctantly, he left his new treasures and trotted off to find Fred. He zig-zagged through the Indian exhibit and then skirted around some Oriental lamps and folding screens. The carved wooden chairs with dragon heads didn't look like a good place to find Fred. He glanced at the Chinese ginger jars, painted elephant tables, silk pillows, and a giant, GIANT Buddha. Ruffie made a mental note to tell C.C.

"Fred! Oh, Fred! Are you still up here?—Darn it, Fred. Where on earth are you?" Ruffie called.

"That dog!" muttered Ruffie. He wasn't exactly thrilled with this hide-and-seek game they seemed to be playing. Besides, he was also getting worried . . . this floor was like a maze.

As he frantically tore around the last corner, he skidded right into a marvelous library. Ruffie thought he was in *the* White House. The room had a handsome fireplace with bookcases on either side, a coffee table with holiday candles, a Persian rug, leather wing chairs, another beautiful Christmas tree, and . . . FRED!

Funny freckled Fred was stretched out full-length, happily snoring on a long, plaid sofa.

"Wake up, Fred!" Ruffie pleaded. "I've been searching for you everywhere. Now, I'm afraid we might be late. And, oh-oh! Look at your black and white hairs all over the cushions!"

"(Gulp!) I sure hope that elevator is working," said Fred, meekly.

It was.

CHAPTER FIVE

Tʜᴇ ꜰɪꜰᴛᴇᴇɴ ᴍɪɴᴜᴛᴇꜱ were up and the little group was gathering back on the first floor. Yvonne, C.C., Monica, and Snow were impatient to tell about their "fabulous finds" and were fidgeting with excitement . . . especially Yvonne, with her very, very own surprise.

"Where ᴀʀᴇ Fred and Ruffie, anyway? We should never have let those two go off together," said Monica.

"Well, I just know it's Fred's fault," snipped Yvonne. "He just loves to roam around . . . that was the problem at his old house." Yvonne was about to lose her usual good humor.

ꜱᴡᴏᴏꜱʜ, ᴄʟᴀɴᴋ. The elevator door opened and out charged the two rascals.

Ruffie wasted no time, "Okay, everybody, tell us what you found and which was your favorite?"

They all started jabbering at the same time.

"Whoa, Pahdners! Hold up y'all! One at a time, please. We'd better go alphabetically," hollered Fred, barely heard above the racket. (Fred just realized that he had less than twenty-four hours to practice his Texas drawl.)

"I guess I'm first then," said C.C. "You won't believe your eyes when you see all the sparkling things on the second floor. My favorite would probably be the big glass bowls. Or the doves. Or—oh, I can't decide. Maybe, the mice."

"Ha, ha, ha! Such a Smarty-Cat," howled Snow.

"Well, Ah'm next" said Fred, "and Ah found at least 2,000 sofas and chairs to jump on. Ah was just gettin' warmed up when Ah found a right nice library with mighty comfy furniture. There was even a real ol' fashioned Christmas tree with lights and everythang." (This dog's new Texas accent sounded a little odd to all his San Francisco friends, but they were much too excited to tease him about it right then.)

Monica sprang nimbly onto the closest gift table. Her sunshine-yellow eyes were larger than ever. "There's a whole, big room of just jewelry," she squealed. "Pearls, jade, gold . . . and there are even stuffed animals wearing expensive earrings and necklaces locked in the display cases. Come see for yourselves. It's just incredible."

"Whoopee," whooped Fred.

"Fan—tastic," shrieked C.C.

"A-maz-ing," purred Snow.

"Gump's is amazing. And we're only halfway through our sharing." announced Ruffie.

Waiting her turn was almost too much for Yvonne. Of all times to be a "Y."

Then Ruffie straightened up, as tall as a tabby cat with long legs could, and said, "I found a wonderful art gallery on the third floor. My favorite thing would be to pretend I'm a docent and take you all on a guided tour. There's a whole bunch of interesting art work, sculptures, and paintings. Even a room full of Indian things from New Mexico. And . . . ."

Snow couldn't wait either. "My turn, my turn," she interrupted by grabbing a Japanese parasol and twirling it over her head. She started right in describing some of the curious foods from Europe and here in California. "My favorites were the funny, brown balls called 'chocolate truffles'; maybe we could even play some games with them later on."

Then Snow laughingly turned to Yvonne: "I do believe you're next."

Her turn at last! Yvonne remembered to take three deep breaths to calm herself. "I just happen to have the really very, very best idea . . . ." She spoke clearly and slowly. "Why don't we celebrate our own special Christmas right here inside the store?"

Their five enthusiastic cheers could be heard outside on Post Street.

Fred, Ruffie, Monica, C.C., and Snow were jumping up and down and congratulating Yvonne all at the same time.

Yvonne continued, "We can draw names for the gifts; there must be something in the Fancy Food Department for our dinner; we can open the presents and sing carols in the library; and then (Yvonne took another deep breath) we can go down to the second floor and have our family Christmas dinner. I saw tables already set for a holiday party."

"Will we have to put the presents back, Yvonne? Or can we take them with us to our new homes?" asked Monica.

"Well, Monica, I think the most fun will be shopping for just the perfect gift. And don't forget everyone, it's really the thought that counts! Then first thing in the morning, we can put everything back where we found it."

"This will be our farewell dinner, too," Yvonne added softly.

CHAPTER SIX

SHOPPING FOR the perfect present turned out to be the most fun of all. Yvonne was right.

Monica took only a few minutes to decide on a pair of gigantic, clip-on earrings for Yvonne. That was easy. Yvonne had the biggest ears she had ever seen.

C.C. remembered something on the second floor. He retraced his steps and picked out a fire-engine red tie for Fred. Clever Cat laughed to himself as he wrapped a red string around the box. At least, Fred could keep the string and wear it as a tie at one of those dress-up, Texas bar-b-cues.

Yvonne drew Ruffie's name and soon found just the right gift for a traveler. Miniature world globes from England that had been made into book ends. One would be enough she thought; they weighed a ton!

Ruffie scrambled back up the stairs to his art gallery and picked out the smallest of his favorite prints. Surely, Snow would like to see the famous St. Andrews Golf Links in Scotland!

Snow was so pleased with her funny idea for Monica, she headed straight for the Jewelry Department. But when she got there, Monica was already picking out Yvonne's earrings, so she quickly hid behind a red poinsettia plant. When the coast was clear, Snow went right to the watches. Most were too fancy, but she finally found a plain one. The perfect collar for a curious cat who was seldom on time.

Fred was stumped . . . what would C.C. like? He vaguely remembered boinking through an Oriental display, so he sniffed his way back and grabbed a bright blue pillow with tassels on the corners. It was the exact color of C.C.'s eyes.

CHAPTER SEVEN

ONE BY ONE, six clumsily wrapped presents appeared under the Christmas tree in the library. Then, one by one, the little pals arrived in the Fancy Food Department on the first floor to do their "grocery" shopping.

This turned out to be quite a challenge. Everyone, except Ruffie, thought the names were confusing and the food kind of strange.

There were so many things to choose from: canned oysters and liver pâté (pat-aye) from Fauchon's (Foh-shone's) store in France, thin crackers called flatbröd (flaw-bruh) from Norway, and Stilton cheese from Fortnum & Mason's in London, to name a few.

Good sports . . . they laughed and joked and pestered poor Ruffie.

He was their only expert, and they begged him to teach them more about these new foods.

"What are h-u-î-t-r-e-s?" C.C. spelled out for Ruffie.

"That's French for oysters, C.C., and you pronounce it 'wee-truh,' by the way," Ruffie answered.

"Well, do you think we would like some pâté, Ruffie?" asked Monica.

"Sure, if you like goose liver it might be okay," Ruffie gagged.

"I suppose *biscotti* is Italian for biscuits," said Snow.

"That's right, Snow, but be careful because some are sweet cookies with nuts and some are other flavors, like cheese," explained Ruffie. "See that brown bag, 'Biscotti al Formaggio?' *Formaggio* (for-mah-gee-oh) means cheese in Italian.

Just in case you're interested, *fromage* (fro-mahge) is cheese in French. Or did you already guess that?"

Ruffie couldn't help adding, "Here are two more easy ones for you to remember. Chocolate in French is *chocolat* (show-koh-lah) and lemonade is *limonade* (limm-oh-nahd). Don't you feel smart knowing a few words in other languages?"

HUÎTRES   PÂTE   BISCOTTI   FLATBRÖD   CROUTONS   ESCARGOTS

"Would you please open this bag, Ruffie," asked Yvonne. "The label has a picture of toast squares called *croutons* (crew-tawns), and I'm starving."

Ruffie was beginning to think more about his dinner and less about teaching, when Fred asked, "Say, Pahdner, would we like some of these-here *escargots* (ess-car-go)?"

"Well, I doubt it, Cowboy. They're just plain old garden snails in a yucky, garlic sauce. Some of that turkey and smoked ham sounds pretty good, though."

At least they could always take the dishes of pet food from their windows if they didn't get enough to eat, Ruffie thought to remind everyone.

"Yum, look over there! English plum pudding for dessert," pointed Yvonne.

"That's jolly-good for an Old English sheepdog. Your sunglasses sure are a big help, Yvonne!" Now Ruffie was getting silly.

"And, please don't forget my chocolate truffles!" Snow was getting silly, too.

"Now, we're all set," said Yvonne, and she ran ahead to choose just the right table with her favorite blue and white plates. After all, wasn't this her very own, grand idea?

Everyone helped carry.

C.C. and Monica added the final touch: they found a drinking fountain in the employees' lounge and carefully squirted water into six crystal goblets!

40

CHAPTER EIGHT

Yvonne, ruffie, C.C., Monica, and Snow scampered merrily up to the
library and watched as Fred turned on the Christmas tree lights and the
electric fireplace. The perfect setting for their family party.

Next, Yvonne led a rousing chorus of "Jingle Bells" to get everyone
in the holiday spirit.

Suddenly, even the library had come to life and seemed
to be smiling and hugging this lucky little group.

And, what fun they had opening their
presents! Just what they had always
wanted, of course!

Saving her favorite Christmas carol until last, Yvonne asked all her friends to hold paws and she led them in softly singing "Silent Night, Holy Night."

These happy sounds of oohing and aahing, laughing and singing floated out into the deserted store . . . and there they lingered, long after Fred, Yvonne, Ruffie, C.C., Monica, and Snow had gone.

Downstairs at Yvonne's festive table, Christmas at Gump's was a huge success—even though the menu was a bit unusual and they did have to put back their wonderful presents.

Ruffie spoke for them all when he raised his water goblet and made this toast:

"To old friends—to new adventures"
Fred leapt up and quickly added: ". . . and three cheers for Gump's and the S.P.C.A.!"

44

CHAPTER NINE

SOON THE LITTLE circle of friends was puzzled by a strange feeling of being both happy and sad at the same time. Yes, their wishes for new homes had come true; but, surely, they would miss being together.

Fred, looking at these happy-sad faces, suddenly burst out laughing! "Guess what Ah forgot to tell y'all . . . Ah overheard my new owners telling the children that the whole family would be driving out to Disneyland and San Francisco next summer. And, if the twins behaved themselves, Yvonne and I could come along, too. So, see! We'll all be together again real soon!"

"I just thought of something else . . ." added Yvonne, "Haven't we also given each other a truly wonderful Christmas gift? A gift we can keep forever—the gift of friendship!"

And so, the two dogs had made certain everyone was smiling again.

With their magical Christmas almost a memory, Fred, Yvonne, Ruffie, C.C., Monica and Snow hugged each other good-night and found a comfy sofa, a chair, or a crystal bowl for their last night in Gump's.

Except for Snow, who crept back to her favorite spot . . . the miniature four-poster bed in the moonlit window.